For Frank and Amanda
- C.L.

For Mom and Dad
- J.M.

LITTLE TIGER PRESS
An imprint of Magi Publications, London SW6 6AW
www.littletigerpress.com

First published in Great Britain 1997
This edition published 2003

Printed in Dubai
1 85430 937 4

1 3 5 7 9 10 8 6 4 2

Clever Little Freddy

by Christine Leeson

pictures by Joanne Moss

LITTLE TIGER PRESS

One crisp, star-frosted night Mrs. Fox gathered her three cubs together outside the den.

"I think it's time you all learned to hunt," she told them. "Tonight I want you to try to catch your own dinners."

Franny and Benny were very excited. They frisked
and jumped and raced into the woods to stalk mice.
But they were clumsy and noisy and they didn't catch
a single one. Benny even got bitten on the nose.
"*I'm* not catching any silly mice," said Freddy. "I'm much
too clever to bother with all that chasing. I'll let my supper
come to me."

Freddy trotted through the woods until he reached the road. His mother had often told him not to go there, but Freddy knew there were sometimes tasty treats alongside it. A car sped past. Something pale and fluttering flew out of its window and landed at Freddy's feet. Was it alive?

It didn't move, but it smelled delicious. It even *tasted* delicious.

"What a clever fox I am!" cried Freddy. "I've found dinner without having to do any work." And feeling very pleased with himself, he trotted home.

"Well, how did it go?" asked Mrs. Fox
when the cubs returned to the den.
Freddy stepped proudly forward with his catch.
"That's *human* food!" cried Mrs. Fox.
She glared at Freddy, but she couldn't
be cross for long. There wasn't much
meat on the worm or the beetle
that Franny and Benny
had caught.

The next morning, Mrs. Fox sent her cubs off again. This time Franny and Benny hunted pigeons, but the big birds easily flapped out of their way and perched in the trees. Franny tried to climb after them.

Freddy could hardly stop laughing
when Franny got stuck and Benny
had to help her down again.
"Too bad you have to work so hard
for nothing," he called. "As for me,
I'm going to find myself another
easy meal."

Freddy wandered down to the riverbank.
A fisherman sat there with a picnic basket
by his side. Freddy knew he should stay
away from people, but the wonderful smell
coming from the basket was too much to
resist. He waited until the fisherman dozed
off and then crept up to the basket.
Just in time! As Freddy slinked away with
a sandwich, the fisherman yawned and
opened his eyes.

"You tried your best," Mrs. Fox was telling
Franny and Benny when Freddy returned home.
They had brought her a snail and a tail feather.
"Look what I've got!" said Freddy.
"That isn't *prey*!" cried Mrs. Fox. "You didn't hunt it."
"I sneaked up on it ever so quietly," said Freddy.
"You're too clever for your own good," said Mrs. Fox.
But Freddy didn't hear her. He was too busy taking
another bite.

The next evening, Mrs. Fox sent the cubs out to catch rabbits. Off went Franny and Benny into the fields, where the rabbits' white cottontails shone like stars in the dusk.

Benny followed one of them down a rabbit hole and got stuck. Franny had to pull him out by the tail.

Freddy shook his head. "I'm not going to waste my time catching rabbits," he thought. "*I* know where there's even juicier food."

Freddy trotted toward the farmyard. He had heard it
was a dangerous place, but when he peered through
the fence he could see a nice, plump gosling.
"Yummy!" thought Freddy. "Just waiting for me."
Very quietly, he crawled toward the gosling . . .

one step . . .

two steps . . .

three steps . . .

Suddenly, everything happened at once. The gosling squawked. The farm dog barked, and all the other geese came running toward him, hissing and honking and snapping. Freddy was terrified and looked for a way to escape. He saw the gate and dashed out as fast as his four paws could carry him.

He raced along until he reached the woods.
The geese and the dog were close behind
him, and Freddy thought his last moment
had come. But then something happened.

A streak of red fur launched itself on the pursuing animals, barking and snarling. There was a flurry of fur and feathers, and in a moment Mrs. Fox was beside Freddy.

"Run, you silly little fox, run!" she cried. On and on they ran, until the noise of the geese and the dog was far behind them.

At last Freddy and his mother arrived home.
"What did you catch this time?" asked Franny.
"Freddy nearly got caught himself," said Mrs.
Fox, and she told them what had happened.
"Poor Freddy!" laughed Benny and Franny.
"Serves you right for being too clever."
"Time for bed now," Mrs. Fox said, giving Freddy
a lick, "before you get into any more trouble."
Freddy crept into the corner of the den and lay
down. Soon he was eating sandwiches again
— but this time it was only in his dreams.